Eenie Meenie HALLOWEENIE

Written by Susan Eaddy   Illustrated by Lucy Fleming

HARPER
An Imprint of HarperCollinsPublishers

Eenie
meenie
Halloweenie.

Kitty, bat, or snake?
Perhaps a bear?
I might just wear
a costume that I make.

I have some tights and turtlenecks,
some headbands, tape, and glue.
My dress-up trunk is full of things
that I can try on, too.

A **penguin** would be fun to make, dressed up in blacks and whites.

I'd put on Daddy's tux and shirt

and wear my orange tights.

Or what about an elephant?
I could be one of those.

With pillowcases for my ears,
a sock could be my nose.

Eenie

meenie

Halloweenie . . .

pig or chimpanzee?

A sweater and a mask would make . . .

a monkey out of me!

This fuzzy-wuzzy coat could be
the perfect thing to wear.
With paper ears, I'd turn into . . .

A big pink **polar bear!**

I might just be a **turtle**
with my shell shaped like a dome.

The laundry basket that I'd wear
would be my mobile home.

Or I could be a little snail,
whose neck is long and skinny.

A blanket roll could be my shell,

pipe cleaners for antennae.

A rhino or an ocelot?

Giraffe or kangaroo?

Eenie
meenie
Halloweenie . . .
I know what to do!

At last!

It's here!

It's Halloween!

I'll shout out, "Trick or treat!"

My candy sack is BIG because . . .

My wild things have to eat!

For Lynn and Lee
—S.E.

For Rebecca
—L.F.

Eenie Meenie Halloweenie
Text copyright © 2020 by Susan Eaddy
Illustrations copyright © 2020 by Lucy Fleming
All rights reserved. Manufactured in China.
For information address HarperCollins Children's
Books, a division of HarperCollins Publishers, 195 Broadway, New York, NY 10007.
www.harpercollinschildrens.com

ISBN 978-0-06-269167-5
Library of Congress Control Number: 2019941382

The artist used Photoshop to create the digital artwork for this book.
Typography by Rachel Zegar
20 21 22 23 24 SCP 10 9 8 7 6 5 4 3 2 1
❖
First Edition